The Wand 2

Lilly's Story

Written by

Robin Bee Owens

Illustrated by

Christopher Bramer

BOCH Publishing LLC
BOCH Publishing edition / August 2019

ISBN-13: 978-1-949350-12-8

Special thank you to all of the fans that loved The Wand and asked for another one. This book is for you all, especially for my mother.

Table of Contents

Chapter 1: **Not a good childhood**

Growing up in an orphanage is hard for any child, but it is especially hard for Lilly. She feels like she isn't good enough for anyone to love, even by the adults that ran the home.

All of the children in the home are without parents. They hope someone will come and take them away. They want someone to love them. They want a family they can call their own.

Each week, Lilly lines up with the other children to meet the people that come to find a child to love. Each week, another baby or toddler is adopted, over time, Lilly sees her chances getting slimmer and slimmer for her turn.

Every night, Lilly lays in bed and thinks back to her early childhood. The memory of her mom is dimming, but she can still see her brown hair and her form sitting in the rocking chair. She remembers the books her mother read to her. She remembers her long, tapered fingers as she points to the butterfly on one of the pages. A tear slips down her cheek as she thinks on these things.

She hits her pillow hard, fighting back the tears, "Why did she have to die and leave me all alone?" She plops back down and turns over, trying to get the sleep that continues to escape her.

Tossing and turning, Lilly's mind goes back to the day she came here. The men and women that came to her house were all wearing uniforms. One lady stooped down to Lilly's level and started talking to her.

"Hi sweetie. What is your name?"

"Wiwwy."

"Hi, Lilly. How old are you?"

"I am four years old."

"Wow, you are a big girl, aren't you?"

Lilly nods her head. She sees a big bed on wheels come into the house and sees her mommy being taken out in it.

"Where is mommy going?"

"We have to take your mommy, sweetie. She has gone to be with the angels. Do you know what that means?"

Lilly shakes her head.

"That means your mommy went to sleep and won't wake up."

"I can wake her up! Mommy! Mommy!"

"Lilly, do you have a grandma that we can call? Where is your daddy?"

"I don't have a daddy or a grandma."

"Ok sweetie. Come with me. We need to find a place for you to stay."

That is the day Lilly becomes a resident of Westover Orphanage and she has been here ever since. One more year and she is out for good. School ends in two weeks and she will graduate. She can get out and be on her own.

Chapter 2: Graduation

Senior year in high school flies by. One moment you are going to your first day of school and the next you are graduating.

All of the seniors were bustling with excitement as they stand in the common area, all wearing their cap and gown, waiting to walk across that stage and receive their diplomas.

Lilly is thinking of the day she will move out of Westover and into the campus dorms at one of the several colleges that accepted her application. It helps that Lilly is the valedictorian of her high school and that she has a 4.5 GPA. She won't have to attend too many years in college because she also took classes at the community college in town while in high school.

Lilly glances at her watch and realizes that the music will start in five minutes. She will lead her class into the auditorium and will be sitting in the front row. She knows that there will be no one in the audience to watch her or to support her. A tear falls down her cheek and she brushes it off very quickly. She thinks of her mother and wonders if she will be proud of her.

The music begins and the guidance counselor wishes all of them congratulations. She marches in with the principal and assistant principal along with some of the teachers and senior advisers. Then it is time for the students. Lilly leads the way and stands there until the row she is in is filled, then she sits with the rest of them. The last student comes in and that row sits down.

The senior advisors come to the podium, one by one and gives a brief speech. Then it is Lilly's turn. She stands before her class and looks around at them. A couple of the kids live at Westover with her, but the rest of them are turning around in their seats and waving to their family members that are sitting in the audience.

Lilly begins her speech:

"Many of you, sitting here, have family members and friends sitting in the audience. You know they are so very proud of you, as they should be. There are a few of us that have no family here, no friends, no one to celebrate this time with us. That may sound very sad to you all, but it is ok. We have each other. Most of us grew up together, going to elementary school, through middle school and high school and here we are, at our graduation. We are celebrating this together.

Some of you are going to take some time off of school and go on to work, some will get married and have children. Some of you will join the military and serve our great country and some of you will attend college; whether it is a community college or a university. You all have dreams for your future.

When we come back for our ten year reunion, most of you will be extremely successful, some will have children getting ready to go to school, some will have lived all over the world and some will still be working, not really knowing what they want. That is ok. It is your life, you get to choose what you want. Some will have passed due to illnesses or accidents. We will remember them fondly, wishing we had kept in touch with them.

Life will fly by now. You will be amazed how quickly ten years, twenty years and even thirty years go by. You will think back from time to time and wonder what ever happened to Lisa or Roger. You will think of your instructors and wonder what they are doing with themselves now that they have retired. You will read in the paper one day that one of them has become a City Counselor or a State Senator. Time will go on, day after day, hour after hour. The important thing to remember is to make good use of each moment.

The only one that will get in the way of your dreams for the future, will be you. If you want something bad enough, you will find a way to achieve it. Be happy with your choice. If you are not sure what you want to do, think about what you enjoy doing. See if there is a career field that will incorporate that.

So as we graduate today, think of how much work you put in to getting here. You will realize you have to do better than high school and put more effort into your future. Go be the best that you can be. Success is an individual thing. Only you will know if you are successful.

I leave you with these words, go be as successful as you want to be. Thank you and congratulations to us all."

The class stands and the applause sounds like thunder in that small auditorium. The principal stands and he gives one last speech.

One by one, beginning with Lilly, the names are called, diplomas are given, family shouts out and flashes of the camera go off rapidly. Life is about to begin.

In the front of the school, Lilly sees the family members taking pictures of their graduate. She briefly thinks of her mother once again. Wishing she could have been here. She smiles at her fellow classmates and turns to leave.

Chapter 3: Lilly Falls in Love

Campus life is more than Lilly hoped. Life, for the first time since she was four, was normal. She has a couple of good friends and she is dating a wonderful man. His name is Richard Bradford and Lilly is so much in love with him. Even her friends are envious of her. For Lilly, life is good.

Richard is in his senior year and Lilly is now a sophomore. They meet at the pep rally the school is having for their homecoming football game. For such a small woman, she has a set of lungs on her and could match the cheerleaders in the victory cheers. Richard sits behind her and watches as she gets into the cheers and the celebration. He has never met someone with such spunk.

After the rally, he walks up to her and introduces himself. Being slightly embarrassed, she shyly introduces herself. They talk for a while and Richard asks if she will come to the football game with him. She accepts.

Since that night, the two have been inseparable. Even when Richard graduates and attends the law school nearby, you will see Lilly on his arm, all over town.

Lilly meets Richard's parents and is invited to come to church with them. She accepts. While in church, Lilly sees genuine love. She hears of Jesus and God and learns how much they love her. She decides to continue going to church. Each and every Sunday, Richard and Lilly ride up to the church and meet up with Richard's parents. They greet the others in church and sit down to listen to the sermon. Some of the parishioners hear Lilly singing during the praise and worship section of the service and they approach her about joining the choir. She loves singing and decides to do this. "Finally," thinks Lilly, "I have a family."

Life is really good.

Lilly wakes up on the eve of her graduation. She looks at the calendar and wonders where time has gone. College is almost over! Graduation is tomorrow. Lilly is totally blown away on how fast these last three years have gone.

"Richard" Lilly says, as she paces her room talking to him on the phone. "I cannot believe this day has come. Graduation. Now what do I do? I haven't heard back from any of the schools that I applied to. I don't know if they have hired any teachers for the positions yet!"

"Calm down, Lilly. It is going to be ok. You will be called and you will teach. I have been praying for you."

"Ok, I will try to calm down. I just cannot believe I will no longer be a student. You will be there, right?"

Robin Bee Owens

"Lilly, I wouldn't miss this for the world. My parents will be there too. Just calm down, ok." Richard says this with a chuckle in his voice. "I am so proud of you and cannot wait to see you march across that stage."

It is graduation day. Lilly reflects back on graduation from high school and then thinks of this graduation. She feels more excitement about this one because she has people in the audience that is there to support and cheer for her. She crosses the stage with a little more pep in her step. The moment the degree is placed in her hands she feels that there is nothing that could make the day better for her. She found out later that was totally wrong.

After the graduation, standing outside with Richard and his family, she hears a commotion and turns her head to see what is going on. It is a group celebrating because they gave their graduate a brand new car. Lilly turns back around and see Richard on one knee. *"What is he doing?"* asks Lilly to herself.

"Lilly. I love you with all of my heart. Will you marry me?"

"What? Marry you? Wow! Yes, I will! I love you!"

Richard slips the ring on Lilly's finger. She looks down at her hand and sees a ½ carat diamond, on her finger.

"Oh my goodness! Oh my goodness!" Lilly exclaims with tears in her eyes. She then squeals really loudly and shouts to her few friends that were standing nearby. "I'm getting married! I am getting married!"

Her friends came running over, looked at her ring and gives her the biggest hug. They shake Richard's hand and congratulate the both of them. This is the best day in Lilly's life, so far.

Chapter 4: The Wedding

Lilly loves her life now. She is teaching kindergarten in the elementary school down the street from her home. She sings in the choir at church and is busy with getting things ready for the Easter Cantata. Richard is finishing up his law school and is scheduled to take his board examination in a little over a week. Once he receives his license, he will be employed by Edward and Wright Law Firm.

A date is not set for their wedding. They both agreed to wait until he has his license and is at the law firm. Then they will start looking at the calendar and setting a date.

Lilly sits at her desk in the spare room, preparing her lesson for tomorrow at school. She wants to help the children learn their alphabet and not just memorize them. Tomorrow's lesson is on the letter H and she is making a huge, hairy H. The children will help name the letter. She loves her job. She sits back and starts daydreaming of being a wife and of having children. "How many children do I want? One, two maybe three?" she thinks out loud. "I wonder how many children Richard wants. This is something we have never discussed. I will make sure to ask him tonight, while we are at dinner."

Lilly looks at her clock and realizes that she needs to get ready. She stands up, stretches and walks out of her office and into her bedroom. Looking through her closet, she picks out a flowing green sundress and a pair of green and yellow pumps. She lays these onto her bed and goes into the bathroom to take her shower.

After a nice hot shower, blow drying her hair and getting dressed, she puts on the last touches of make-up when the doorbell rings. Trying to get to the door while putting on her pumps and putting in her earrings proves to be a bit of a challenge, but she gets it done. Opening the door, she sees Richard. He is smiling from ear to ear and has a bouquet of flowers in his hands. "*How corny but super sweet,*" Lilly thinks to herself.

"Hey Richard. Come in. I have a little more to do and I will be right with you. Will you put those beautiful flowers in the vase for me? I have one on the counter." Richard looks at her and frowns.

"What's wrong?"

"You didn't kiss me, hug me, thank me or say I love you. You just say hey and put the flowers in the vase. Hmmm...not even married yet and you act like we are." He chuckles when he sees the look of fear in her eyes.

"I am so sorry. Let's start again. Go back outside and we will try this again..."

Richard doesn't let her finish. He grabs her and kisses her.

At dinner, Richard looks at her and says, "We need to set that date."

"I thought we were waiting for you to pass your exam and start working?"

"We did. I did and I am."

"What? When did you take the test? I thought that was in another week or so!"

"We were given a practice test. Those of us that got a 97% or higher would be given our license. The board is using that as our test as well as the school using it as our final exam. I have my license and I talked to old man Edward and he was impressed. I start working on Monday. Like I said earlier, we need to set that date."

Lilly didn't care where they were or who was around. She jumped out of her seat and gave Richard a big hug. "I am so proud of you."

They did a little more talking. Lilly is excited to know that Richard wants as many children as she wants. He would love to see a houseful of little girls and boys running around the house. Lilly thought about this and said that two would be plenty. They laugh and talk well into the night. Lilly knows she has to get home because she has a classroom full of kindergarteners to teach in the morning. Richard gets her home, gives her a hug and a very passionate kiss and they say their good nights.

14

Lilly looks at her calendar. Six months is not a long time to plan a wedding. Thankfully, they will be having the wedding in his parents' backyard. They live in the country and are surrounded with the forest. The colors should be perfect for the day, middle of autumn.

For the next several months, Lilly is busy with all of the wedding plans. It is to be a simple wedding, nothing extravagant. One of the ladies in the church is a photographer. After speaking with her, she feels confident in having her take the pictures. She also was given an excellent deal, half off of the prints and services will be a gift to her and Richard.

Also, in their church, another couple have their own catering and bakery business. They told Lilly and Richard that as a wedding gift, they will provide the cake and the catering is at 20% over their cost.

Lilly is overwhelmed with all of the generosity of the people in their church.

Next on the list are invitations and the counseling with their pastor. They need tables, chairs and floral arrangements. Her dress, the dress for her maid of honor, which is her close friend and dorm room mate, Elisa, is also on the list. They need to go shopping and find these. Even with all that needs to be done, everything is falling right into place.

"One week before the wedding!" Lilly screams as she paces back and forth. "One week before the wedding and now you tell me you cannot be my maid of honor! Elisa, I do hope you have a very good excuse for this? Oh my heart, I cannot take any of this stress. Not this close to the wedding!"

"Lilly, calm down. I do have a good reason. Now listen to me. I cannot be your maid of honor, because you see, Pete and I eloped last night. So I cannot be your 'maid' of honor. I can, however, be your matron of honor."

"What! Pete and you eloped! Elisa! Why didn't you tell me you two were planning this!?!" Lilly ran and gave Elisa a hug. "I should smack you because you scared me to death! I am so happy for you. Congratulations!"

The day is finally here. Lilly is excitingly getting ready with Elisa's help. The dress is a simple, straight white gown with long lacy sleeves. It has a sweetheart neckline that is edged with lace and a veil that is so long that it drags behind her on top of the train of the dress. Satin flat shoes adorn her feet. Lilly feels like a fairy princess, she is a vision of beauty.

Elisa's matron of honor dress is tea length, autumn orange color beauty with a sweetheart neckline as well. Orange satin pumps perfectly matches the dress and looks wonderful on Elisa's feet. The color looks magnificent against her dark skin and her hair is swept up in a bun with small orange mums circling around it like a halo.

The music begins. It is time. Lilly stands around the corner in the back waiting to march through the garden. Since she has no one to give her away, that question has been removed from the ceremony.

Richard anxiously awaits to see his bride. His dad is his best man and they both look dashing in their black suits. His dad is wearing an autumn orange vest and matching bow tie. The color matches Elisa's dress perfectly. Richard is wearing the same color bowtie and a matching cummerbund.

Lilly rounds the corner and starts walking down the makeshift isle that has been made in the garden. Richard gasps as he sees her. He is sure that he is seeing an angel. How can someone so beautiful be marrying him.

Lilly is smiling as she watches Richard. She is so happy. She is not only marrying a man she loves with all of her heart, she is gaining a family of her own.

Chapter 5: Baby Makes Three

"Are you sure?" Lilly asks the doctor.

"Yes, Lilly. You are definitely pregnant."

Lilly thinks of how she will tell Richard. It is their second anniversary, so it will make a wonderful gift for him.

"Doc, can you give me a copy of the results with the word 'pregnant written across the bottom in large letters?"

"Yes, I can do that. What are you up to, Lilly?"

"Today is Richard and my anniversary. I want to place it into a card for him."

"Most definitely. Happy Anniversary. I will have my secretary make a copy of this report for you. I will personally write the results on the bottom. Tell Richard that I say, congratulations."

"I will, thanks Doc."

Doctor Williams is a member of Richard and Lilly's church. He is also their Sunday school instructor and he sings in the choir with Lilly. Lilly sees him as a father figure since she never knew her dad, he was never in the picture.

That evening, Richard comes home with a bouquet of flowers for Lilly. When he walks into the house, he sees the table is beautifully set, with candlelight. He is caught off guard. He thought he was taking her out for dinner.

"What's this, Lilly? Aren't we going out for dinner?"

"I thought we would have a private celebration. Is that alright with you? Oh, Richard, the flowers are beautiful!"

"They are beautiful, but they pale in beauty next to you."

"You always know the right words to say. I love you."

"Happy Anniversary, sweetheart."

Richard puts his arms around Lilly and passionately kisses her. His kisses always makes Lilly swoon. How can anyone be so much in love? She is amazed at the love she feels for him.

After dinner, Richard hands Lilly his gift. A locket. A beautiful locket with his picture. She loves it. She jumps up and gives him a hug. "Thank you, Richard. I will cherish this always."

Lilly hands him a card. "What, no gift!" Richard says with a wink. He loves teasing her because every time she asks him what he wants for his birthday or for Christmas, his answer is always "you."

She sits there, waiting anxiously for him to open the card. She is bursting at the seams to shout out that she is pregnant, but she controls her urges.

"What's this?" Richard asks as he opens the paper that is inside the card. He looks at it, sees the word at the bottom, shakes his head and looks at it again. Then he looks at Lilly and looks at the paper again. "What! Lilly! Are you serious?"

Lilly doesn't know if he is happy or upset. She sits there just looking at him. She is afraid that he is upset and didn't know what she was going to do if he was. Then she sees his smile widen. He gets up and gently lifts her to her feet. "This has to be the best present ever. I am so excited. We are going to have a baby!"

Lilly is relieved and a tear forms at the corner of her eye. Richard hugs her tightly, but not too tightly now because he feels she is delicate.

The weeks and months pass by quickly. Richard pampers Lilly throughout the pregnancy. He will get up at two in the morning to go to the store and get her chocolate peanut butter candy, or even look everywhere for pickles, hamburger, whatever she is craving. He makes sure she has it and then some.

"Richard! Richard!"

"Lilly!" Richard calls out as he runs to their room. "Where are you?"

"In the bathroom!"

Richard walks in and sees water all over the floor. "What happened?"

"My water broke."

Richard helps Lilly change and gets her into the car. He runs back in and grabs the suitcase they packed a week ago so that it will be ready when the time came. He cannot believe the day is here. He wastes no time getting to the hospital, without breaking any traffic laws.

Cynthia Joyce Bradford makes her appearance at three thirty in the afternoon, weighing in at six pounds and eight ounces and twenty inches long. She has a head full of black hair, dark eyes and a set of lungs that can be heard half way across the hospital. Lilly is exhausted but full of joy and Richard is beaming. They cannot believe how beautiful their daughter is.

Chapter 6: Cindy

Time flies when you are an adult with a child. One moment, Cindy is making her entrance into the world and the next she is going to school. Where did the time go?

Lilly is so involved in Cindy's life, a hands on mom. She makes sure she is in church and Sunday school every week and she has her involved in the program at church for children. They meet every Sunday evening while the adults have Bible study. Life is so good.

Cindy is seven years old now. She will be having a birthday in a couple of weeks. Lilly is busy getting the party together. All of the invitations are ready to be given to the children in church, the cake is ordered and the decorations are sitting in hers and Richard's closet.

Lilly thinks back over the last eight years. The joy of waiting for their little girl to make her entrance and the joy of seeing her grow up. The first steps, the first words and even the first fall off of her bicycle. Scraped knees that she would kiss and make better, the fight with a girlfriend that Cindy was sure was the end of the world. Lilly smiles at all of this and decides to look at the pictures in her album.

She opens the first page and sees her as an infant. All dressed in pink with a bow headband on. Such a sweet looking angel.

The next page is Cindy as a toddler. Her first steps recorded forever to enjoy. A picture of her favorite stuffed giraffe. "She still takes that giraffe with her everywhere she goes." Lilly says out loud to no one.

The next page is her first day of pre-school. She looks so proud in her new dress and her ballerina backpack.

After reminiscing for some time, Lilly puts the album up and looks at the time. "Oh my, is it that time already? I need to get to the bus stop."

Cindy gets off of the bus and Lilly gives her a big hug. "Mommy, I can't breathe." Cindy says.

Lilly laughs and steps back. "Ok, ok. Just know I love you to the moon and back kiddo."

"I love you too, mommy."

Back at the house, Lilly gives Cindy a snack while she sets up at the table to do homework. While working on the assignments, Lilly begins dinner.

At night, Lilly and Richard sits and listens as Cindy tells them about her day. She settles down with her Bible story book they got her for Christmas and reads to them. Tonight is about Noah's ark. She loves this story and how the dove comes back with an olive branch.

The day of the party is a success. The kids all enjoy the games they play and the cake is a hit. Lilly and Richard cannot believe their baby is now eight years old. Pictures are taken to keep record of this forever. Little did Lilly know that this will be the last birthday pictures she will ever take.

Chapter 7: World Upside Down

The day starts off like any other. After church, Richard takes Cindy shopping so she can spend some of her birthday money. Lilly begins making the cookies Cindy is to take to church for a party they are having.

She puts the batch in the oven and hears the car drive up. She waits to hear the door open and listens for the squeals of Cindy telling her everything she bought.

She hears footsteps to the door and then the doorbell chimes. "Why would he ring the bell, he has a key," Lilly says out loud to no one. She opens the door and starts to speak, but is brought to silence as she stares at the two officers standing at her door. They have something in their hands, but Lilly cannot process what it is that she's seeing. The first officer asks her if she is Mrs. Bradford.

"Yes," she says with a tremor in her voice. "May I help you?" Just then, she recognizes the stuffed giraffe in the second officer's hand. "That is Cindy's giraffe! Where did you get that?"

"Ma'am, do you have someone with you right now?"

"No."

"May we come in?"

"Yes." Lilly is feeling like someone is pulling strings making her move. Much like a puppet. She steps aside and lets the two officers in.

"Ma'am, would you please have a seat?" asks the second officer.

"Why? What's wrong?" Lilly's legs are shaking badly right now and her heart starts to palpitate. She sits in her chair.

"Ma'am, there has been an accident. Your husband and your daughter…"

Lilly doesn't hear anything else except the timer going off. She gets up and walks without thinking to her stove and turns off the timer. She opens the oven and takes out the cookies and turns the oven off. She is on autopilot. "*There's been an accident*" is going over and over in her head.

"Where is my daughter and my husband?"

"Ma'am, we need you to come with us to identify the bodies."

"Bodies? What bodies?"

"Ma'am, there has been an accident. Your husband and daughter were both killed."

"NOOOOO!!!!" screams Lilly. "Get Out!!! They are not dead!! They will be coming in at any moment. Cindy needs to get dressed for a meeting at church. She has to take the cookies with her."

"Ma'am, we need you to come with us."

Lilly starts screaming and then everything goes black. She wakes up seeing the first officer standing over her.

"Ma'am, ma'am. Wake up."

Yes, wake up Lilly. This is all a nightmare. She closes her eyes and shakes her head back and forth.

Lilly doesn't remember much after that day. It is all like a dream from which she cannot wake up. After the funeral for both her husband and her daughter, she sits in her rocker, crying and praying. She is not understanding why she lost both of her loves.

Her whole world has turned upside down.

Chapter 8: The Wand Appears

Life is so hard for Lilly. She feels so alone. She feels God has turned His back on her. She cries all day, every day until there are no tears left.

This morning, Lilly drags herself out of bed. She passes Cindy's room and the tears start flowing again. She goes back to the bedroom and picks up the stuffed giraffe and hugs it to her. She mopes around in one of Richard's shirts. To say Lilly has hit rock bottom is putting it mildly.

"Why God? Why give me a family just to take them away from me? Wasn't it enough that I had no family when I was a child? Why take my family from me?"

Lilly goes into the kitchen and grabs a knife. She has it pointed to her stomach and screams out. "Why didn't you take me too? Why leave me here, all alone? Well, take me now?"

Just as she finished saying this, she sees something glowing on her sofa. She puts the knife down and walks over to see what it is. "A wand. Where did that come from? It has to be Cindy's. I don't remember Cindy having a wand?" Lilly looks at the wand very closely. It has a gold star on the top, the shiniest gold she has ever seen. The handle is crystal with gold flecks inside of it. The bottom has a pearl ball. The prettiest pearl ever.

She sits in her chair and just stares at the wand, all day. She finally gets up, throws the wand in the garbage and heads to bed for another restless night.

The next morning, when she gets up, she sees the wand. It is back on the sofa, right where she found it the first time. Again, she throws the wand into the garbage, takes the bag out of the garbage can and places it into the bin, right outside her house. She dresses and starts cleaning house. When she finishes, she sits in her chair and sees the wand again. On the sofa, once again, right in the same spot.

"What is going on here? I threw that thing away several times already, why does it keep showing up?" She picks it up, carries it right outside and throws it into the garbage bin again. When she goes in, not only is the wand back, but there is someone standing there, all dressed in white, holding it.

"Don't throw this away, Lilly. It will lead you to a gift from God."

"Why would God give me a gift? He took away the only gift that meant anything to me!" Lilly shouts at the man standing there.

"This will lead you to a gift that will last you forever."

"Who are you?"

"I am Gabriel. I am a messenger of God."

Lilly shakes her head. "I must be dreaming." She says.

"No, Lilly, you are not dreaming. God sent me to give you the wand and to tell you that this will lead you to a gift." Gabriel says this as he fades away.

Lilly stands there looking at the wand. She is wondering what gift God is sending her. How can an object lead her to a gift from God? Lilly is about to find out.

Chapter 9: Life on Her Own

It has been a year since the accident and Lilly is working very hard to adjust to life on her own. The wand is on her coffee table, where she can see it every day.

This morning, Lilly wakes up and realizes she finally had a good night's sleep. No nightmares, no tears, just much needed sleep.

After getting out of bed and making it up, she goes into the kitchen to make coffee. "It is time I think about what I want to do with my life."

She picks up her notebook and a pen and sits at the kitchen table, with her coffee in hand and starts writing down a plan of action for her life.

First, I need to go through everything in this house and take care of Richard and Cindy's clothes and personal items. People in our community can use these things. It is time I let them go. Lilly knows that will be the hardest thing to do, but it is time to clean.

Second, I need to get back to church. I haven't gone since the accident except for the funerals.

Third, I need to find something to keep me busy.

Fourth, I need to make a doctor's appointment to have my yearly check-up. My doctor has been after me for a year now to come in.

Lilly continues writing down everything she needs to accomplish. She has been doing this for four hours now. When she looks up at the clock, she jumps up and starts working on checking off on the list, in no particular order.

She picks up the phone and calls her doctor's office. The receptionist was so happy to hear from Lilly. She asks how she is doing and then schedules the appointment for her. "We look forward to seeing you again, Lilly."

Lilly thanks her and puts the date on her calendar. She then grabs some boxes out of the garage and goes into her bedroom. "It will be easier to work on Richard's things first." Lilly begins in his closet. Every suit she takes out, she hugs it, smells it and remembers what he looks like wearing it. She then folds them neatly and places them in the box. The shirt she takes out was very special to her. It was the shirt he wore the day Cindy was born. Lilly realizes she cannot get rid of this shirt and decides that she will keep it and wear it as a nightshirt. "*It was his favorite shirt,*" Lilly thinks to herself. Next were some personal items that belonged to Richard. His wedding band she places in her jewelry box. She cannot bring herself to part with that one. "Maybe I can have a piece of jewelry made from it for me."

After everything is done, Lilly has six large boxes of clothes, two boxes of books and another box of law books. She decides that she will take the law books to his office and let his partners have them. The rest of the boxes she will take to the mission house in town. The men that stay there, looking for work so they can get a home of their own, they can use some of these to help on their interviews for employment.

Lilly takes the boxes, one by one and loads up the car with them. The legal books are the last to be loaded and is placed in the front seat. "I will take all of these tomorrow."

"I am hungry." Lilly looks at the clock and realizes that she has been cleaning for several hours. It is well past dinner time. She looks in the cabinet and finds a can of soup and some crackers that have not been opened. After warming this up, she sits down, says grace and then begins eating.

After eating dinner, Lilly picks up her Bible and starts reading it. This is the first time she has picked the Bible up during this difficult time in her life. She decides to read Psalms.

Chapter 10: Getting Back to Normal

Sunday morning comes quickly when you start getting your life to a new normal. Lilly puts on her dress, applies her makeup and fixes her hair. She grabs her Bible, her purse and her keys and heads out of the house. This is the first time back to church since Richard and Cindy died.

She walks into the church building and the pastor sees her right away. He walks right to her and hugs her. "Lilly, I am so happy to see you back in church. We have missed you."

"Thank you for all of the phone calls and visits, Pastor. I wish I could say I was a good hostess, but to be honest, I don't remember much of this last year."

"That is understandable. Is there anything we can do for you? Do you need help with anything?"

"I cannot think of anything right now, but I will let you know the moment I think of anything."

"You do that. I will let you get to your seat. I see a line of people wanting your attention before service begins. It is great having you back with us."

"Thank you."

Lilly finds a seat and has difficulty sitting. So many of the members comes to her and start hugging her. The chatter was nonstop until the music started to signal the start of church.

The singing of the choir makes you feel like you are hearing a host of angels sing. The sermon is a good one, from the book of Daniel. A story Lilly remembers Cindy reading to her and Richard from her Bible story book. The faith Daniel shows by not giving up on praying. He continues to talk to God even when it becomes illegal to do so. For his faithfulness, when he is thrown into the lion's den, God sends an angel to close the lion's mouths. Even though these lions were starving, they do not harm Daniel. The king is overjoyed when he sees that Daniel is alive. He has him taken out of the den and throws his accusers in. They are eaten right away.

God is always faithful to us. We are the ones that need to work on being faithful to Him.

The invitational hymn is beautiful as it always is.

Lilly starts to leave when Julie, the choir director, comes to her and asks her to come join her for lunch.

"Thank you, Julie. I will need to take a rain check if I may. I have more things to go through at home."

"Would you like some help?"

"No, I need to do this myself. Thank you again."

Julie hugs Lilly and lets her go.

After getting home and having a glass of lemonade, Lilly gets to work in Cindy's room. This takes longer than it did going through Richard's things. Lilly will cry over every little thing that she picks up to pack away. The one thing she cannot part with is Cindy's Bible story book. She knows that another child will benefit from this book, but she just cannot let it go. And she cannot give up Cindy's giraffe.

It takes Lilly several days to go through everything in Cindy's room. When she packed the last item in a box, she starts loading up her car. She plans to drive to Westover Orphanage and donate the items there. She is sure there is a little girl that can use the clothes and the children will love the toys. Plans have a way of changing at the last possible moment.

The pastor calls her and tells her of a fire that took away everything a young family in their church owns.

"They are all safe, but they have lost everything. I am calling all of our members and regular church goers to see if they may have anything they are able to part with to help this family out."

"Pastor, I just finished cleaning out Cindy's room and was about to drive to Westover Orphanage to donate her things. This family has a daughter about Cindy's age and I think she should have them. Should I bring these boxes to the church? To you? Where should I take these items? There are clothes, books and toys in these boxes. I also have all of her bedroom furniture if one of the members can come by and pick that up."

"Oh, Lilly, what a blessing! I will have Joe and his wife come by tomorrow for the furniture. They can also pick up the boxes as well if you want?"

"They are all already in my car. I can be at the church in ten minutes."

"Ok. I look forward to seeing you. Thank you, Lilly. You will help bring a smile to this little girl."

Lilly hangs up the phone and goes to the car. She takes the boxes of Cindy's things to the church where the pastor and the dad to the little girl help her unload. The dad cannot stop thanking Lilly for this act of kindness for his little girl.

The next morning, Joe and Lisa, his wife, come to Lilly's for the bedroom furnishings. Lilly also gives them the bed sheets, pillows, blankets and comforter. She throws in the matching curtains and the book cases, desk and toy box. Joe is amazed at how much Lilly is giving them to take to this family.

After everything is cleared out of Cindy's room, Lilly sits in the middle of the floor and starts crying. She misses her baby girl and her husband. She really doesn't know how she is going to make it without them.

Sunday rolls around and Lilly is dressed and ready for church. Today, she decides to go back to Sunday school.

Standing in the hall, she isn't sure which class to go into now. Richard and her attended the couple's class together and have made many friends in there. But she isn't a couple any more.

The singles class are mostly college aged students. The widows class were women twice her age or more. She turns to leave when the pastor sees her.

"What's the matter, Lilly?"

"I don't know which class I should be in."

"What about the widow's class. The ladies would be totally understanding of your situation."

"I could, but they are all twice my age if not more."

"Hmmm…I see your point. Why don't you go on to your old class for today and we can talk after church this afternoon."

Lilly walks into her old class. The people all gathered around her, hugging her and telling her how much they have missed her. It is nice to be with friends, but Lilly feels so lost without Richard by her side.

After another wonderful sermon on the Tower of Babel, Lilly stays behind to speak with the pastor.

"Lilly, we have a need here in church and I was wondering if you will be willing to fill that need?"

"What is the need?"

"We need someone to take over the nursery during the Sunday school hour. Karen is moving and there is no one that has stepped up."

Lilly thinks on this a moment. This could help fill the void she fills inside. "Sure, Pastor. I can take the nursery."

"Great! I will let Karen know that we have found her replacement. You can start next Sunday. You will work with Karen for a couple of weeks to see how things are done."

For several months, Lilly works in the nursery. She loves being with the toddlers. They bring such joy into her life. But, she still feels a void.

Chapter 11: The Void

Lilly fills her every waking moment with something to do. She goes back to work, even though she does not have to. She takes classes on drawing, painting, and knitting, anything to keep busy. But she still feels a void in her life.

She attends church every Sunday morning, Sunday night and Wednesday night, but there is still a void. She doesn't understand why she feels so empty inside.

"Maybe it is time for a change" Lilly thinks to herself as she picks up a real estate magazine at the grocery store.

Once home, Lilly gets all of the groceries put away and makes a pitcher of lemonade. Once that is done, she pours herself a tall glass and sits in her chair. She takes out the real estate magazine and starts looking through the pages. There are a couple of cute houses, but nothing jumps out at Lilly. She puts the magazine down and gets ready for the new painting class that is starting tonight.

Sunday comes so quickly these days. Lilly loves Sundays. She loves going to church to be with her friends. The sermon today is on the birth of Jesus. Lilly loves this story. It is the reason for her favorite holiday, Christmas. She listens as Mary is visited by the angel, telling her that she will have a child. She thinks back to the day she found out she was pregnant and smiles. She listens to the story more intently than ever before. She did not realize that Mary had not been with Joseph yet. She didn't really take in before the fact that Mary was a virgin.

After going home, Lilly sits down and pulls out her Bible. She rereads the passage the pastor read today in church and then went a bit further. She reads how Joseph puts Mary away and then is visited by the angel telling him that it was ok. That Mary was still untouched. The baby she was carrying is from God. He is to be the son of God and his name is to be Emmanuel. Lilly closes her Bible and thinks on this. She knows that in that day and time, if a woman is pregnant out of wedlock, she is usually stoned. If she is engaged, or betrothed, the man can have her put away instead of stoned. Joseph must have really loved Mary to prevent her from being stoned.

Lilly looks at the time and sees that it is time to get ready for church again. She gets up and runs a comb through her hair. She touches up her makeup and heads out of the door.

The sermon tonight was a little more in depth of this morning's message. More on what she read this afternoon.

After church, Lilly goes home and starts to feel the void again. She sees the wand on her table and picks it up, looking it closely and thoroughly. She thinks back to what Gabriel said about the wand leading her to a gift that will last for eternity. *"I wonder what that gift is,"* Lilly thinks to herself. She heads into her bathroom and showers and gets ready for bed.

That night, Lilly tosses and turns. She dreams of the day the police officer came to her door. She wakes up screaming. It felt so real. She lays there crying.

An hour later, Lilly finally gets up from bed and dresses for work. She went back to teaching kindergarten when Cindy began school. She always enjoyed being in her class, teaching her students; but the joy has gone out of teaching since the accident.

It is to be a short day at the school, only a half day. Lilly gets to work and sets up her class for games. There is no need for a full lesson today being it is only a half day, so Lilly decides to play games as a way of instruction.

After work, Lilly stops by the grocery store to pick up the new edition of the real estate magazine. She has been doing this for some time now. She decides that a new home would be better. Maybe that will help fill the void that she feels in her soul. She feels the house holds too many memories to be happy.

Lilly gets home, fixes a sandwich for dinner and pours herself a tall glass of lemonade. She sits down and starts looking through the magazine. A house jumps at her. It is a bit of a drive from her community, but it is the perfect little cottage. She picks up her phone and calls the real estate agent listed on the cottage.

She picks up the wand again and looks at it. Maybe this is the gift Gabriel is talking about. Maybe it is a fresh start, in the country. Some-where, where she isn't reminded of Richard and Cindy every second of every day.

Chapter 12: New Life

Lilly meets the real estate agent to see the cottage she had found.

"Oh, how cute!" Lilly exclaims as they drove up.

When they make it to the cottage, Lilly is pleasantly surprised by what she sees. A cute cottage, in a clearing, smack dab in the middle of the forest. Made of stone, cute shutters and what really sets it off is the front door.

"I have never seen a door shaped like a heart before." Lilly states.

"It does give it that extra charm, doesn't it," the agent replies.

They step inside and Lilly falls in love with the place instantly. A very cozy looking living room with a fireplace on one wall and built in bookcases on either side. An eat-in kitchen straight through to the back of the house and there are two bedrooms to the right of the living room and down the hall. The master bedroom is at the far end of the hall and to the right. It is a nice size bedroom with a huge walk-in closet and a half bathroom and laundry room combined.

The second bedroom is across the hall. It is a nice size room, almost as large as the master bedroom. It has a double closet and a big window seat at the bay window.

The bathroom is on the same side as the second bedroom but closer to the living room. Very large with a garden tub and a separate shower. Very cozy, very cute, the right size.

"This is perfect," Lilly says.

After looking over every square inch, Lilly goes to the realtor's office and places a bid on the cottage. It will take a couple of days to a week to know if her bid is accepted, so Lilly drives back home, which is a couple of hours away.

As soon as she gets into the door and places her keys onto the table where the phone is, she notices that blinking light on her answering machine. Before retrieving her messages, she changes into something a bit more comfortable than the dress she was wearing. She goes into the kitchen and grabs a tall glass of fresh lemonade. Then she checks her messages.

One is from her friend, Elisa. She is checking in on her like she has done for the last couple of years, since the accident.

Then she hears this message. "Lilly, this is Anna with Rowles Realtors. Could you give me a call as soon as possible? Thank you."

"Hmmm…I must have left something in her car or forgotten to sign something." She picks up the phone and dials Anna's office number. "Hello, Anna, this is Lilly. I am returning your call."

"Oh, hey Lilly. Thank you for calling so quickly. I wanted to tell you that the owner of the cottage accepted your bid? This is the quickest I have ever seen a bid go through. He was excited and said yes."

Lilly looks down at the table and sees the wand. She picks this up and then says, "It is God's will. When is closing? Do I have any more paperwork to fill out?"

"I am overnighting the paperwork to you. How about we close in three weeks, pending loan approval."

"That won't be necessary. I will be paying cash. Three weeks will be perfect."

Hanging up, Lilly looks around her house with a mixture of feelings. She is sad to leave her home with all of the fond memories of Richard and of Cindy, but she is happy to start a new life.

The next three weeks, with the help of her church family, Lilly packs up her house. She donates and gives away quite a few items. She hangs onto Cindy's Bible Story book and giraffe and Richard's favorite shirt that she sleeps in and his Bible. Everything else of theirs, she had already donated a while back. She packs all of her books and pictures, knick-knacks and clothes. She writes her resignation for her teaching position.

Exhausted, she sits down in her chair with her lemonade.

She picks up the wand and asks, "Is this the gift? Is this the gift, to start fresh?" She looks around, wondering if Gabriel will show up. He is there but she cannot see him.

"Not yet, Gabriel."

"Ok, Lord, I will wait."

Chapter 13: Moving Day

Lilly meets Anna at the realtor's office and signs the last of the paperwork. She is given the keys and a handshake. With a few items in her car, she heads to her new home.

She takes these items into her new place, the wand is among the items. She places this on a shelf of one of the built in bookcases. It appears to shine and she hears a whisper in her ear. "It will lead you to a wonderful gift."

Lilly is taken aback hearing this. She responds, "Isn't this the gift?"

She looks out of the window and sees Gabriel standing several yards away at the edge of the forest. Then she hears him whisper again.

"No, but this is where God wants you to be. It is a start."

Lilly looks around her. "A start?" she queries. She shakes her head, not understanding. She looks back over to where Gabriel had been standing and does not see him.

"It is a start" plays over and over again in her head. She is now very curious as to what the gift is and how this is a start. She grabs her keys and makes sure the cottage is locked up. She drives back home. Pete and Elisa will be meeting her in the morning to help her move. They have a step van that will be able to hold her furniture and items that she has left.

The next morning, Lilly and Pete work hard loading the van. Elisa cannot lift anything heavy because she is in her sixth month of pregnancy. When it gets time to load up the heavy things, the pastor along with other men from the church show up to help. Lilly uses this time to clean the house good.

While cleaning and talking with Elisa, she asks, "Would you and Pete like to buy this place from me?"

Elisa drops her cloth and says with disbelief, "What?"

Lilly looks at Elisa and repeats her question, "Would you and Pete like to buy this place from me?"

Elisa sits down and looks at Lilly. "Are you serious? How can we afford this place? We have nothing in savings so no bank will lend us the money."

Lilly chuckles. "Elisa, I don't owe a thing on this house, thanks to Richard. He invested some of our money. With the car accident and the settlement I got, plus the investment, I was able to pay this place off and buy that cottage too. I am set for life. I would make it a legal document between us that you would pay me. No banks will be involved."

Elisa jumps up and hugs Lilly, screaming for Pete as she does so. "Pete! Pete!!"

Pete comes running in thinking something is wrong. Elisa tells her what Lilly just suggested to them. Pete is dumbfounded but very excited as well.

Elisa and Pete started talking to each other at once. They were just wondering where they would put the baby in their one bedroom apartment. Now they know.

They settle on a very reasonable price and monthly payment, set up an appointment with an attorney and agree to meet in one week to finalize the deal. Pete cannot believe how quickly God answered his prayers.

After everything is loaded into the van, Lilly looks around and wonders how they are going to get everything unloaded when they get to the cottage. The men of the church told her not to worry herself over it. They were all going to follow them and help unload everything. The only payment they ask for is some pizza and some of Lilly's infamous lemonade.

Lilly is blown away by the generosity of the people in this church and she knew instantly just how much she will miss them. A tear forms on the corner of her eye as she agreed to their terms.

Lilly looks around and says one last good bye to Cindy and Richard. She locks the door and gives Elisa the keys to the house. She figured they could go ahead and start moving in while they wait for the appointment with the lawyer.

The convoy to the cottage begins, with Lilly leading the pack.

Chapter 14: New Home, New Church

Lilly gets settled in. She met with Elisa and Pete at the attorney's office and they all signed the paperwork. She had to fill out a promissory note and sign it. Elisa and Pete also sign the note and then they gave Lilly a hug. They cannot believe their good fortune at having a home where they can bring their baby to.

Lilly leaves and on her way to her new home she feels the void again. This is a void that cuts deep into the soul. She doesn't understand what it could be.

"Church," Lilly says out loud. "I need to find a church."

She gets home and looks in the phone directory to see if she can find a church close by. Her home is now thirty minutes on the other side of town and she wants to find something a bit closer.

There are several churches listed. One is on the edge of town and the others are either in town or on the far side. Lilly decides to try the church on the edge of town. "*I can use the time after church to go get a few items I need from the grocery store or department store.*" Lilly sets the directory down and makes a glass of lemonade.

She takes a walk outside and looks around her property. She sees the perfect spot to plant a garden in the spring. She looks at the front of the house and decides that a nice flower garden will look perfect next to the house and along either side of the walkway.

After her stroll, she goes back inside, fixes a small dinner and then decides on a shower and then she goes to bed. It has been a very exhausting few weeks.

Lilly wakes up and gets ready for her first visit at the church on the edge of town. She is a bit nervous but the excitement takes over. She looks at the wand as she heads out and wonders when she will find that gift Gabriel has been telling her about.

Lilly pulls up to the church and is taken by its old world charm. A brick building with a steeple and a cross on top of that. Double wooden doors at the front. She walks in and sees the charm continuing. Knotty pine planks from floor to ceiling with stained glass windows on both sides. The wooden pews line both sides of the sanctuary and at the front is a handmade table and pulpit. Behind the pulpit is the choir loft with the baptistery behind that. The picture for the baptistery is a scene that you would expect to see at a river. Very quaint and really beautiful.

Lilly finds a place about midway to sit. She doesn't sit for long when people takes notice of her and go meet her. Hand shake, introduction and questions, which is how it starts for her.

The organ begins to play and everyone finds their seat for service to begin. After opening with prayer, the announcements are given. Next is a song from the old hymn books on the back of each pew. Welcome to visitors, more singing, the offering then the choir sings. After this is done, the pastor goes to the front and begins his sermon.

The title of the sermon is "Where are you going?"

"Interesting title" Lilly thinks to herself, as she takes out her Bible and notebook.

"If you look around on any given day, you will see loads of people heading for somewhere. Some are going to school, some to work and some to do the grocery shopping. Going to the doctors, dentist or even to the gym. Someone is always going somewhere. Where are you going?

Even in the Bible, the people were always going. Moses, going to Egypt to get his people out of bondage, Noah going onto the ark to escape the flood, the apostles going into all of the world to spread the gospel.

Even in spirituality, men are always going. For example: Romans 10:3 says 'For they being ignorant of God's righteousness, and going about to establish their own righteousness, have not submitted themselves unto the righteousness of God.' We see this more and more today.

Did you know, and this may apply to some of you in here today, there are people in this world that try to establish their own righteousness just by attending church? Yes…there are many, who has heard the gospel preached, has read about it in the Bible and still think that by coming to church, they are Christians and 'hope' to go to heaven when their time comes. Unfortunately, many of these, when their time comes will find themselves in hell instead.

In Matthew, the Lord tells us this. Matthew 7:14. Turn there with me if you have your Bibles with you. If you don't have a Bible, we have copies in front of you, on the back of the pews.

Matthew 7:14 tells us 'Because strait is the gate, and narrow is the way, which leadeth unto life, and few there be that find it.'

Let's look at the verse before that one. Matthew 7:13 tells us 'Enter ye in at the strait gate: for wide is the gate, and broad is the way, that leadeth to destruction, and many there be which go in there at:'

You see, few will be going into heaven and many will go into hell. Where are you going?

The Bible tells us how we can get to heaven. I will give you the ABC's of blessed assurance of spending eternity with our Lord.

Admit: Admit that you are a sinner and in need of God's forgiveness.

Romans 3:23 'For all have sinned and come short of the glory of God.'

We cannot say we are good enough. Coming to church does not make you good enough to go to heaven. You have to admit that you will never be good enough compared to God. And honestly, that is the type of goodness needed to be in heaven, to be compared to God. You have to admit that you are a sinner, you need God to forgive you for your sins. All sin. Even a little white lie is a sin. Anything that goes against God is a sin. We are all sinners.

Believe: Believe that God loves us so much that He sent His only begotten Son, Jesus Christ to be born of a virgin, to be crucified on the cross for all of the sins of the world, including yours and mine, and He rose up on the third day from the grave. Believe this in your heart, in your mind and in your soul.

Romans 5:8 'But God commendeth his love toward us, in that, while we were yet sinners, Christ died for us.'

Confess: Confess our sins to God. He may already know them, but He wants you to come to Him and confess to Him.

We are told in 1 John 1:9 this 'If we confess our sins, he is faithful and just to forgive us our sins, and to cleanse us from all unrighteousness.'

That is the only way we can get to heaven. To have him forgive us for our sins, to cover us with His blood.

How can you forgive someone unless they come to ask for the forgiveness? God does not push Himself onto us, He is willing to forgive us, but we have to ask him.'

So we have a choice. We can come to God and ask Him to forgive us, or we can choose to ignore this and continue to think we are Christians because we go to church.

Let me ask you a question. If I came to your house, stood in your garage and say I am a car, does that make me one? No. Well, this is the same thing. We can come into God's House, but unless we go to God and ask Him to forgive us, we cannot call ourselves Christian.

Where are you going? Heaven or Hell. Only you and God knows this one. I will be here, at the front of the church. If you have not admitted to being a sinner, believed in the birth, crucifixion and resurrection of His Son and confessed your sins to Him, then, my friend, I have bad news. If you left here right now without doing this and you get hit by a car and die, you will going to a place called hell that was originally designed for Satan and his followers. It will be too late then. If you cannot think of a time that you did admit, believe and confess, maybe not the exact day, but you cannot recall a place or time period, I beg you to come forward today. Don't hesitate. Come to the Lord and have blessed assurance that you will go to heaven. As we sing, don't hesitate, come."

The pastor steps down from the pulpit as the organ plays the hymn "Blessed Assurance." Lilly thinks on this sermon while they all sing and realized that she has never heard anything like this. She has never come to God for forgiveness. She believes in Him, but she never asked Him to forgive her. Lilly steps out and heads to the front.

The pastor smiles as he shakes her hand. He listens to her and calls his wife over to sit with her and talk to her. She and Lilly walk over to an empty spot on the front pew and she shows Lilly from the Bible how she can be sure of salvation. Lilly bows her head and prays: "Lord, I have never heard this before. I know the pastor at my old church had to have taught it, but I never heard it. I know I am a sinner Lord. I know that compared to you, I deserve to go to hell. I also believe that you sent your Son, Jesus, to take those sins and to have them nailed on the cross with Him. I should have been the one to die on that cross, He did not deserve that, but I am thankful He did. I also believe that He defeated death on the third day and that He arose from that grave and is now seated at your right hand. I am asking you to forgive me. For every sin I have committed, whether in thought or in deed, I am asking for your forgiveness. Come into my life, Lord. Fill this void which I now know is there because you aren't. Come fill this void. Let me be a child of yours. Thank you, Jesus, for dying in my place. Thank you for rising up and giving me hope. I pray this in Jesus' name. Amen."

Lilly feels the void leave her. She feels so happy right now. She feels light. She has more confidence than she has ever had. She now knows that no matter what the future holds, she is going to be alright.

At home, Lilly sits down with a tall glass of lemonade and smiles. She knows where she is going and that is the best feeling in the whole world.

Chapter 15: Renewed Life

Since accepting the Lord, Lilly has been the happiest that she can ever remember. She is baptized two weeks after accepting the Lord.

While cleaning the house, Lilly notices the wand is gone. "Where did that wand go?" She looks under the table that it sat on. She looks on the bookcase and all around the living room. Into her bedroom she goes looking for the wand. "Where is it? Where is the wand?"

Just as she examines every corner of every room, she enters the living room and sees Gabriel standing there.

Being startled at first and then with a chuckle, Lilly says, "Hi Gabriel. It is good to see you again."

"Lilly, what are you doing?"

"I am looking for the wand. I cannot seem to find it anywhere."

"The wand has done what it was sent to do. It has led you to the greatest gift from God."

"What? You mean it is now gone?"

"Yes, the day you accepted God's gift of eternal life, the wand was taken back to heaven."

"So, that is the gift? You are right, it is the best gift ever. Will I ever see the wand again?"

"You never know," Gabriel says this as he fades away. "You never know."

Lilly stares at the spot where Gabriel was standing for a moment longer. She shakes her head, walks to the kitchen for a fresh glass of lemonade and returns to her seat to read her Bible. She finds that she gets more from the Bible these days and reads as much as she can. She spends time in prayer too.

"Lord, I ask that you show me how I can serve you, today and every day."

This is a prayer Lilly starts her day with.

The cottage is beginning to take shape. She has flowers in window boxes all across the front of the house. In the back she has a vegetable garden. This morning, she goes out and sees the beginnings of her tomato plants. She looks at this in awe and then looks up to the heaven. "Thank you for this beautiful plant and this beautiful day." She looks back at the new plant and it hits her. She is able to think about Cindy and Richard and smile now. She no longer cries. Her depression has been taken from her. And the void? It is gone as well.

Chapter 16: God Answers

It has been five years. Five years since accepting Christ. Lilly cannot believe how quickly these five years have gone by. She catches glimpses every so often of Gabriel and gets a message. "The Father is watching you and He is very proud of you."

Each time she hears this, she smiles. "Thank you, Father," she would respond as she looks up to the heavens. She still asks Him to let her know how she can serve Him each and every morning.

This morning, Lilly gets up, says her prayers. She makes her bed, cleans her bathroom and after getting dressed, goes into the kitchen for breakfast. She has a feeling that something important is about to happen, but cannot find anything on her calendar.

After cleaning house, she goes to her garden to pick some of the beautiful tomatoes and cucumbers that are ripe. She takes these to her kitchen and slices them up to have with her boiled egg. "What a wonderful breakfast this is. Thank you, Lord, for another beautiful day and for this food that I am about to eat."

All of her chores are done for the day and fresh lemonade is made and in the refrigerator, Lilly makes a glass for herself and sits down to read. She adores reading. Today, after reading the Bible, she picks up a book about Abraham.

She hears a knock at her door. Putting the book down, she arises to answer the door. At the door is a beautiful girl, about fifteen, with blonde hair. Lilly looks at what the girl is holding and what she sees, surprises her. It is the wand. This girl has the wand.

"May I help you?"

Mary is startled momentarily before she speaks, "Oh, I am sorry to bother you, but I found this wand back at the creek and wondered if it is yours?"

Lilly looks at Mary and is reminded of her daughter Cindy. *"Cindy would have been about this age."*

"It does look familiar, but no, it isn't my wand."

Lilly looks past Mary and sees Gabriel at the edge of the forest. She instantly knows that God has led this girl to her.

"Oh," Mary says, as she turns to leave. "Sorry to have bothered you."

"Don't let her get away, Lilly." Lilly hears this whispered in her ear.

"You didn't bother me. Would you like to come in for a glass of lemonade? I haven't had anyone come see me in such a long time and would love to visit."

Mary steps into the house and as Lilly closes the door, she looks over to the edge of the forest and watches as Gabriel disappears.

www.ingramcontent.com/pod-product-compliance
Lightning Source LLC
Chambersburg PA
CBHW060236180626
46813CB00007B/3110